LOVE FOUND

Jo & Laurie - A Reimagined Little Women Sequel

TAYLOR CLAREMONT

CREEK BOUND BOOKS

Contents

Dedicated to my two little women who help me believe in the magic of this world every day!

Introduction

This book is a love letter to Little Women by Louisa May Alcott, the beloved saga spanning one harsh year in the life of the March sisters. It begins during a penniless Christmas without their father and the curtains close the following Christmas, with an entire year of mischief, heartbreak, fun, and miracles in between.

At the time of this writing, Little Women has continuously been in print for over 154 years! It has touched readers' hearts for generations upon generations and with movie adaptations reviving the story every so often, it shows no signs of fading from memory.

My own beloved daughters and I read one chapter of Little Women each night and after three weeks of delightful joy sending us off into slumber, I checked out the reviews for Good Wives. There I saw a running theme amongst them that could be summarized into one sentence: "I wish I could go back in time and never read Good Wives!"

Not wanting to ruin the idyllic feelings that Little Women created within us, we agreed we'd live as though it were a standalone novel. (We've already made this mistake in the past with our beloved Anne Shirley and would give anything to go back and only know the first in her series!)

Unrequited love can be deliciously indulgent to read about, but in a story where the two characters clearly love and adore each other unconditionally, it makes no sense and almost feels cruel.

Louisa May Alcott did not want Jo to marry at all and it seems as though she had Jo reject Laurie to stick it to readers who wrote to her incessantly asking who Jo would marry, but this book answers the question, what if she said yes to her heart?

I hope you enjoy reading it as much as I enjoyed writing it!

~ Taylor

PROLOGUE

S UMMER *1869*

"Three cheers for our favorite boy!" cried Amy.

"Hip, hip, hooray!" The Marches and Mr. Laurence cried out in response.

Jo beamed with unabashed pride at her Teddy, standing before them looking much as he had the day he started college, but with a certain matureness in his eyes that competed with the sparkle of mischief they always held.

Lively talk amongst the dinner guests resumed and Jo slipped away silently. The summer sun was low in the sky, casting long beams of light through the windows of the Laurence home. Jo ran her finger along the banister Teddy had slid down so many times in their youth. The corners of her mouth tugged upwards at the memories.

"Hey there," a soft voice said from behind her, causing her to stumble.

"Teddy!" she cried, smacking his arm. "Why would you jump out and scare me so?"

"I hardly jumped out. Are you crying?"

Jo wiped at the corners of her eyes and shoved him away from her. "Never. I would never cry, especially when someone might catch me."

Laurie sat on a step and sighed. "I would hardly think less of you if you did." He patted the step, and she freely joined him.

"If I need to cry, I will. I'm not afraid to."

Laurie threw back his head and laughed. "Now that's a fine fellow. Getting offended at the thought of being caught crying *and* at the thought of never being caught crying."

"Why aren't you in celebrating with the others?"

"Why would I celebrate in there when the person I most want to be with is right here?"

"Laurie—we can't—"

"Jo, we have to talk." At this, Laurie gathered Jo's hands in his and looked into her eyes as she shook her head vehemently back and forth.

"No, please don't."

"I've been patient. I've sat back and waited—and I'm fine waiting—but I need to be heard. Give me that, please, Jo?"

When she didn't protest, but sat patiently, he continued. "I am certain I've loved you since the first moment I saw you."

Jo fought the urge to argue and squeezed his hands instead. He took this as reassurance to keep going.

"I cannot imagine anyone I would rather spend my life with. When I think of my future, you're always in it."

"No, it doesn't have to be like that."

Laurie looked at her strangely. "Like what?"

"We don't have to get married to be in each other's lives. If you think you must tie me down in order to keep me, you're wrong. I'm yours forever and ever."

"I'm not saying this out of some need to *tie you down*. I mean it when I say that I want you to be my wife."

Jo's breath caught in her throat, and the room began spinning about her. She planted her feet more firmly onto the ground and leaned her head against the banister.

"I'm sorry, Jo. I know these talks are hard for you, but when I'm around you, it feels as if my heart were about to burst out of my chest and I can't contain it any longer."

Jo exhaled slowly and lifted her head so she could look Laurie in the eye. "I know, dear Teddy. Marriage seems such a far-off and distant thing to me. I see Meg and she is so happy with Brooke and I sometimes wonder if I too want that."

At this shocking admission, Laurie had to steady himself. A flat-out rejection had been all he expected to hear from Jo. Instead, the sweetest words he could have expected came out of her mouth.

"So, you'll consider it?" he asked, getting too excited and too ahead of himself.

Jo scrunched up her face. "Well, no. I didn't say that. Oh, Teddy. I'm not ready for marriage yet."

Laurie clutched Jo's hands and jumped up, pulling her to her feet as well. "Jo, that is the best answer I could hear from you. There's no other woman for me than you, and if I have to wait all of my days, then that's what I'll do."

Jo sighed and pulled her hands out of his grip. "When will you see that I'm not worth the wait?" She shook her head. "I can't force you to do or not do anything, but when you die miserable and alone, don't say I didn't warn you."

Beth's head poked around the corner. "Come on, you two! Meg's surprised us with a cake she made to celebrate Laurie and father is about to cut it for everyone."

"Be right there!" gently said Jo, whose voice had softened even more towards her beloved little sister. She turned to Laurie with a heavy heart. "It's rude to end things like this, but we can't make them wait any longer—"

"Friends?" Laurie put out his hand and Jo looked down at it in amazement towards his jovial response to her rebuff.

"Friends!" She put on a resolute smile, clasped her hand to his, and they made their way back to the dining room.

The partygoers began a round of cheering at the sight of the graduate, and Jo slipped into her seat quietly, with no one noticing the strange look on her face after letting her gaze linger on her Teddy for a little longer than normal.

1

NEW YORK SUMMER *1871*

A sharp rap at the door broke through the silence of the room and brought a scowl to Jo's face. She crumpled the piece of paper in front of her and tossed it to the side of the desk. Grabbing another sheet of paper, she scribbled furiously.

Another knock.

"What is it?" she called out.

"I've a letter for a fellow named Jo March?" a familiar voice responded.

Jo rolled her eyes and set her pen down with a sigh. She opened the door with a glare that would have made most guests run away. This one simply slid in through the narrow gap between Jo and the door without a falter in his step.

"What is it, Teddy?"

"That's a fine way to greet your dearest friend in all the world."

"I saw you this morning. It isn't as if we've been parted for years."

"Yes, but I was getting lonely and bored at my apartment and I thought I'd see what you're up to over here."

Laurie glanced over at the growing pile of crumpled papers next to Jo's desk. "Ah, much the same as this morning, then?"

"I can't seem to get the words right." Jo slumped down into her chair and dropped her head into her hands. "I've written and re-written the scenes so many times and I can't get it how I want it. It's as if the memories have left me."

Laurie's face lost all traces of mischief. "Jo, you haven't forgotten her. I promise."

"Yes, Teddy. I have." Jo stared into the fire roaring in the corner. "I was foolish to write a story about my sisters. I can't get any of them right and I know that if I wait for Amy to get back from

Europe, I'll get her right after spending less than a minute with her. Meg, I only need to go visit, but Beth—" Jo's voice caught in her throat and Laurie started forward, but Jo raised her hand. "No, no. I won't cry, but today has been especially hard."

"It's been a year today," said Laurie softly.

Jo nodded and scrunched up her nose. "I thought you had forgotten when you didn't mention it this morning."

"I could never forget." He took Jo's hands into his and sat still while she closed her eyes. "I wasn't sure whether it would upset you too much to mention her."

"It upsets me every minute of every day that she isn't here. Mentioning her would never make it worse."

"Of course. What shall we talk about? I miss her sweet voice and the way she always made me feel like her dearest brother, even when I hardly deserved it."

"You deserved it more than me. I promised to better myself after she left us. I vowed to be nicer and not as cross, but here I am, always annoyed, always perturbed."

"You haven't been that bad—"

Jo scowled at Laurie and then attempted to soften her face. "See? Look at me. You're my only friend in the world and I'm snapping at you because I miss my Beth."

"That's normal, Jo."

"I've tried so hard to be good. I want to be someone Beth would be proud of. Someone worthy of her."

"Extend some of the grace you know she would give you if she were here. Do that for yourself."

"Why would I? I hardly deserve it—"

"Nonsense!" Laurie cried, dropping to his knees at Jo's feet as she looked down at him in alarm. He lowered his voice and shook his head. "I know you don't care about my opinions of you, but Jo, when will you believe me that you deserve all the love and happiness in the world?"

Jo opened her mouth, promptly shut it, and crumpled up the piece of paper she had on top of her stack. She tossed it unceremoniously into the fire and refused to turn back around.

With her gaze set so resolutely on the crackling flames, Laurie knew all hope of any sort of conversation was over. While her face was turned the other way, he quietly pulled out a fresh stack of paper and a new ink pot and set them both gently on her desk.

"Goodbye, Jo," he said, noticing her head bob slightly in response. "I'll light a candle for Beth while I eat my dinner tonight." At this, her head bowed, and he slipped out of her room without another word.

On his way out of the boarding house, Ms. Springer, the head of all operations and, as such, the neighborhood's biggest gossip, stopped him. "Mr. Laurence! How is Ms. March doing today?"

"It looks as if she's still wrapped up in writing her next brilliant novel." Laurie gave the nosy woman a tight smile and slipped out of the house before she could engage him in any further gossip.

Out in the summery air, Laurie looked up at the sky and wished he was back in Concord. A year in Europe left him homesick and he would never regret following Jo to New York, but he silently counted down the days until she said she was ready to go back home.

The people walking about their business swarmed around him as he inadvertently blocked their paths. He mumbled an apology and stepped to the side. Much to his surprise, after seeing the rest of the world and revisiting the places he spent his days as a young child, he missed the slow-paced life in Massachusetts that he had grown so accustomed to.

When he returned to Concord after his year abroad, Jo was all-to-ready to return to New York. Beth had recently left the world and the March family seemed as if it would never recover. Aunt March passed away shortly thereafter and Amy, being the one to inherit most of her aunt's considerable wealth, went to Europe. She dropped hints to Laurie that she would enjoy his company while there, but he couldn't leave Jo behind again.

And then Jo left abruptly one morning, saying her room at Ms. Springer's boarding house was costing her money every day that she wasn't there writing. Laurie stayed with his grandfather until he was too miserable without Jo.

His grandfather, being the wise old man he was, sent Laurie to New York under the pretenses of business dealings, which Laurie was all too happy to do.

After several arguments on whether living in his apartment was a handout, Laurie dropped the futile attempt to have Jo stay with him. He grinned at the thought of the indignation in her face when he suggested the idea so she could save money.

Oh, Jo.

His sweet Jo with the determination of a hundred men and extensively more heart than any of those men could hope to have.

Laurie held open a door for a woman carrying a baby and smiled back as she thanked him. He carried on his way, heading to the park he could sometimes get Jo to visit on nice days.

Birds chirped in the tall trees around him and he strolled alone, avoiding eye contact with happy couples enjoying the fresh weather. He looped around the perimeter of the park and stopped in his tracks when he saw who was waiting for him at the beginning of his path.

Jo put her hand up and shook her head. "I don't want to talk. I need to walk and could hear Marmee in my ear about getting fresh air and not being all cooped up in my room."

"She's a smart woman."

"I said no talking."

Laurie kept a smile to himself and linked arms with Jo. They made their way round the park in comfortable silence for two-thirds of a loop around before Jo made a disgruntled sound and stopped walking.

Laurie swiftly pulled her out of the way of an oncoming carriage and squared her shoulders in front of him. "I do believe this needs to be a conversational walk and not a silent one."

Jo glowered and looked up at the sky, squinting her eyes against the harsh light. "I can't do it."

"The writing?"

"Yes, the writing. This advance I was given to write a full-length novel was a mistake. I'll have to pay it all back and be penniless." She threw her hands up. "Why did I ever think I could do this? I'll have to run off with only my short stories published."

"Jo, that's a wonderful accomplishment by it-self." Laurie's voice was low and soothing, much the same way one would speak to a cornered rab-bit. "Why don't you come stay in my apartment? Then you won't have to worry about money."

As soon as the words left his tongue, Laurie regretted them. Jo pulled herself from Laurie's hold and crossed her arms over her chest. "I will not be a charity case."

"Jo," Laurie pleaded. "It's not like that. You're my family, Jo. Please let me do this for you. You can write me into the dedication of your book as repayment."

"No. I can afford the boarding house for now. I'll just have to figure out how to pay for it in a few months or—" Jo slumped down on the retaining wall that outlined the park's path. "I'll have to go home." Her face was sober and her eyes looked off into the distance.

Laurie sat down next to her and softly petted her back. "There, there, Jo." He continued doing this until her shoulders relaxed slightly and he knew she would be more receptive to his next suggestion.

2

JO JUMPED UP FROM the retaining wall with to-
tal disregard to the startled passersby. Laurie
ducked his head and avoided any eye contact lest
one of the park patrons recognize him. Laurie
had known Jo wouldn't be *fully* open to his suggestion, but he sorely misjudged just how much
it would upset her.

"Go home? That's plainly what I said I *don't*
want to do!" Jo's cheeks flushed, and she turned
away from Laurie, her shoulders raising with each
irritated inhale.

"Hear me out, Jo." Laurie's plain tone effective-
ly got Jo's attention, and she turned to face him.
Her piercing gaze made his thoughts falter, and
he felt his own cheeks redden with anger as he
lost his cool. "I wish you weren't so frustrating!"

He paced the ground in front of her. "If you're having trouble writing here, you might have luck writing up in your old garret. Marmee and your father would count themselves lucky to have you back in their home. They asked about you the entire time I visited last."

"No."

"Think about it, Jo. I'll ask you again tomorrow when you've had time to consider it."

"My answer will be the same, Teddy. Don't ask me again."

Jo turned on her heel and left the park, leaving Laurie standing there alone and unable to avoid every pair of eyes looking in his direction. He dipped his head in greeting to a couple who he had met with in his office earlier in the week. He was fairly certain they hadn't arrived in time to hear any of his conversation with Jo, but he left quickly instead of hanging around to find out.

Ducking into a nearby door, the tension left his body, and he sighed with relief. Bringing up home had been the first part of his plan and, although it hadn't gone well, he was thankful that part was over and done with.

"Mr. Laurence!" The postman's eyes lit up whenever he saw the young man who was never quite comfortable being referred to so formally. "Are we here on business?"

"Not exactly." Laurie rifled through his bag and pulled out a piece of paper. "I have some personal complications I must deal with. Family matters." He jotted down a quick message, got it ready to send off, and handed it to the postman.

Taking the small letter into his hand, the postman tipped his head to Laurie. "I hope your matter settles itself quickly and rightly."

"So do I," Laurie said pensively.

In her haste to block out the rest of the world, Jo shut her door a little harder than she meant to. A sharp knock on the wall made her cringe. Living next door to a cantankerous old man wasn't her favorite state. In fact, it was proving to be rather bothersome.

Her thoughts drifted off to her other old man of a neighbor and her heart yearned to sit in Mr. Laurence's library, watching him write letters for his businesses while she looked through his endless collection of classics and books she had never heard of until laying her eyes upon his copies.

Before she could nurture the thought of seeing her parents and Laurie's grandfather, she shut down the hopeful feeling entirely and tucked it away. Home didn't feel the same the last time she was there, and it surely would feel even worse now. Without Beth laying on the small couch or sitting at her pianoforte, what was left?

Meg was busy with her twins in her home with Brook, Amy had used her inexhaustible new wealth to tour Europe whenever she felt like it, and Marmee and father seemed to have an unquenchable sadness in their eyes that would never leave. It was too much for Jo to handle and, though it was small and lonely, her room in the boarding house gave her space to exist beyond all of that.

At home, she felt empty and worthless. In New York, she felt like she was accomplished, working towards her dream, a—a fraud. She grabbed the top sheet of paper on her desk and read over it as she dropped her bag to the floor. The words were flat and desperately trying too hard to be entertaining. It wasn't real.

Each person she had shared her story idea with had loved it and now that she faced the task of writing it out, all inspiration had left her.

Laurie's words echoed in the silence of her room. He was wrong, of course. Here, she could pretend Beth was too busy with helping someone to write to Jo. No. She couldn't even pretend that. Her Beth would never have been too busy to write to her, no matter what she was doing. She would miss Jo incurably and undoubtedly convince Marmee to take a trip to see her.

Any time Marmee had written to her about coming to New York to visit, Jo had given her a lame excuse about being too busy to entertain any visitors. Certainly Laurie told her the truth and Jo was immensely grateful for Marmee not pushing her further. She was always good at giving Jo her space and letting her work through things. The thought of her sweet, caring mother made her heart ache for home. But no. Going home would only make everything worse. There, it wouldn't be simply hard to pretend, it would be undeniably obtuse to entertain the idea that Beth was simply off doing something else.

Jo wrung her hands, the thoughts swirling around in her mind, driving herself crazy. She sat down at her desk and settled angrily into her nightly ritual of writing, crumpling, and burning.

Once there lived four girls, striving to be little women. Their father was off to war, their mother staying busy helping others.

Jo surveyed the words and stifled a scream. It was no good. She couldn't find the words, no matter how hard she tried. She scrawled the names of her sisters across the page and a tear fell down onto the ink, smudging the end of Beth's name.

Regardless of the sentimentality, this paper did not escape the inferno waiting for it. She crumpled this particular paper up even more tightly than the rest and threw it directly into the flames.

After watching the embers slowly fade to nothing, Jo blew out the candle on her desk and went to bed more conflicted than ever.

3

A NIGHT OF RESTLESS dreams weighed heavily on Jo's mind and she awoke the next morning with the strong resolve she had so missed.

She grabbed her jacket and ran out the door without a single glance in the mirror. She made her way to Laurie's office and frowned when she didn't find him. Her resolve wavered, and she was tempted to head back to her room for another day of frustration and fire when she heard a familiar voice call out her name.

"Jo! What are you doing here?" Laurie ran the last few steps when he saw her and she hid a smile at his enthusiasm.

"Perhaps I was a bit too harsh yesterday. I do understand that you're just an old friend trying to help a fellow out."

"Noted and no hard feelings here." Laurie held open the door to his office and ushered Jo inside. "You saved me a trip."

"I did, did I?"

"Yes. I was planning to stop by and see if you'd join me for dinner this evening."

Jo looked at him quizzically. "For what cause?"

Laurie looked as innocent as his mischievous face allowed, which should be noted wasn't innocent at all. "No particular cause, really. I thought I might make up for irritating you."

"I hardly believe you, though dinner with a friend sounds like what I need to keep my spirits up."

"A long night of writing?"

Jo slumped down in a chair opposite Laurie's desk. "You are correct. And nothing to show for all that work."

"I have some correspondences I must send off right away. After that, do you want to visit the park?"

Jo pondered his question. "No, I must get some more words down on paper if I'm to be at dinner with you tonight."

Laurie nodded and grabbed a stack of letters from his desk. "It would be too much of me to ask you to work for me, wouldn't it?"

"Absolutely." Jo stood up, indignant, and flashed Laurie a smile that made him glad he poked fun at her. "See you later, my dear fellow."

"What was it you were stopping by to see me for this morning?" Laurie, in his haste to smooth it over with Jo, had disregarded how strange it was to find her at his office so early in the day.

"It's of no consequence now. We can discuss it over dinner."

Laurie bowed his head and watched her walk out, hoping that their conversation later in the day would go better than their last several had gone.

He scribbled out letter after letter and tucked them in his bag. Saying a quick word to his receptionist, he left and rushed to the post office.

"Have any letters arrived for me?" he anxiously asked the postman.

"As a matter of fact, one arrived early this morning. This mail system is a thing of beauty. It seems to be from the place you sent a letter off to yesterday."

Laurie greedily put his hand out to accept the letter. He thanked the postman and handed off the letters he had in his bag, avoiding any more talk about the postal routes, although he appreciated their efficiency on this day.

He delicately opened the envelope and peeked inside. When he saw its contents, he put the paper to his chest and closed his eyes.

"Did your family matter work itself out?"

Laurie quietly cursed himself for being so open the previous day and nodded. "It's about to."

"Good luck with all of it, Mr. Laurence. We'll send these letters out right away."

"Thank you, sir." Laurie tipped his head and exited to the street, where the air smelled sweeter than usual and the early summer sun beat down on his black jacket. He didn't mind the heat as he sprinted to his apartment, safeguarding his newly acquired treasure the whole way.

The rest of his day was spent inside, perfecting exactly how he wanted dinner to proceed. The food wasn't nearly as important as the small piece of paper Mrs. March had selflessly sent his way. Though, with its surefire ability to win over Jo, perhaps her reasons were just as selfish as his own.

Laurie wrestled with his thoughts and guilt when he was interrupted by Mary, the women grandfather insisted he hire to cook and clean for him. She greeted him with a bright smile and put his nerves at ease for a moment. "Is Ms. March joining you for dinner this evening?"

"Yes," he said with trepidation that the older woman detected, even if she was careful to keep her face still and practiced.

"Very well, sir. I'll see to it that there's a fine spread of food for the two of you."

He thanked her and stepped into his office. Unfolding the letter that had come from Massachusetts, he hesitated and headed back out into the main room of the apartment.

Smoothing out the creases and careful to not smudge any of the penciled in notes delicately scribbled down by its previous owner, he placed the fragile paper in front of him and opened up the pianoforte to reveal its keys. He had only a few hours to perfect his pitch and win Jo over.

4

— · —

J O RUSHED INTO LAURIE'S apartment like a wind of garden-fresh air. Laurie stayed seated and painstakingly began playing notes of a song that hurt his heart to hear. Music usually brought him so much joy, but the lack of hearing this song in so long added to its haunting charm.

Jo's eyes moved towards the pianoforte and the sight drew her painfully inward. Her face was pale as she connected with Laurie's eyes. He jumped up and guided her over to a chair slowly, carefully helping her find her bearings.

"Why do you have that?" She pointed, but studiously avoided the music sitting on the stand.

"Jo," Laurie started. "I thought it might be good if you return home—"

"So you thought you'd coerce me with Beth's favorite song?"

"Oh, Jo. No. I didn't mean to coerce you." Laurie sat down on the footstool in front of Jo's chair.

"Then why would you get that?"

"I only wanted you to see what you're missing."

Jo sat forward. "I know what I'm missing. I know every morning when I wake up to a house bustling with the sounds of strangers. I know when I go to sleep every night without the sweet sounds of my sisters' voices filling the air with hymns and silly songs. If I make too much noise, the old man next door bangs on the wall. It's quite different from home and makes me quite aware of what I'm missing."

"Jo, I'm sorry—"

"Where'd you get the music?"

"Marmee sent it to me."

"Why'd you stop playing?" She motioned over to the pianoforte and looked at him anxiously.

Tentatively, he stood up and walked over to the bench, turning back around with each step to make sure Jo was serious and not playing a trick on him. She sat patiently with her hands folded on her lap, waiting for him.

As he took his seat, he would have been less nervous in front of an auditorium of musical judges waiting for him to mess up. He stretched his fingers for a moment and dove into the song. Within three bars, he lost himself in the notes.

It was a simple song, a long-forgotten hymn Beth found tucked away in a folder of music many years ago. She added flourishes and notes as she embellished the song and made it her own. Over the years, it became known as *Beth's Song* and no one uttered a word of it once she was too sick to sit up and play it any longer. In her final days, she asked Laurie to play it for her on the rare occasion the house was empty and he obliged, willingly.

Those moments were filled with a bittersweet haze that tugged at Laurie whenever he thought back to them. He was just as guilty as Jo of pressing down his feelings when they were too troublesome to face, and blinked as some of those feelings slipped out onto his cheeks. His eyes filled up too much for him to see the notes in front of him, so he finished the song from memory and sat silently on the bench, unable to turn around and face Jo.

"Thank you." Her soft voice startled him and he shut the keys slowly.

Jo had stood up and walked across the room. He closed his eyes as she laid her hand on his shoulder. "Jo, I promise I wasn't trying to coerce you. I just want to help."

"I know, Teddy. I know I should go home and that's what I came to your office to talk to you about. It's hard to say out loud and even harder to make my feet move forward and take the journey back to Concord."

"I'll be right by your side, my fellow. We shall adventure together and keep each other's spirits high."

"Oh, Teddy. I shall only survive with you next to me. Won't Marmee be so surprised?"

"That she will. Though, I'm guessing she was confident that her gift of this song would bring you home." Laurie stood up and faced Jo. Her eyes were shining with unshed tears, and he pulled her in for a tight hug.

"I do long to go home. It won't be the same, though."

"Nothing ever is," Laurie said with a forlornness that made his throat close on the last word. He coughed and squeezed his friend tighter. "Some of those changes will be good. The twins must be huge by now."

Jo simply nodded, much too overcome to speak.

Mary entered the room to announce dinner and hastily exited when she saw the two embracing. She had grown fond of Mr. Laurence's boy, but she still couldn't understand the strange relationship he had with the March women.

Of particular curiosity were the interactions with the youngest of the girls. She didn't stop by often, but when she did, Mary's master was left unsettled and agitated. He spent days fretting and agonizing over minor details when she left and didn't seem like himself for at least a week.

At least with this one, despite her unruly hair and unkempt appearance, her company seemed to uplift the boy and bring an unextinguishable smile to his lips. It didn't seem to matter that the two saw each other every day. His excitement was palpable whenever he headed her way or prepared for her arrival.

Although she couldn't understand it, Mary could appreciate the love between them and hoped one day they would see what seemed so obvious to the rest of the world. For now, she shut the door to the parlor and kept their food warm until they were ready.

5

"THE JOSTLING OF THIS carriage is not helping my nerves." Jo put her hand to her stomach and looked out at the changing landscape as the city turned to the countryside.

Laurie reached over and clasped her hand. "We can stop as many times as you need."

Jo set her chin resolutely forward and squeezed his hand. "No, I should think I could make the journey without a stop."

Biting back a smile, Laurie settled in more comfortably. "I wouldn't expect anything less."

"Good. I haven't ridden such a long distance in quite a while. I simply need to exercise these muscles, and I'll be unrecognizable on our journey back compared to this paltry state I'm currently in."

"About that," Laurie hesitated. "When do you plan to go back to New York?"

Jo scrunched up her nose. "I haven't given it a proper thought. I paid Ms. Springer through the end of the next two months so she retains my room through summer. I don't want to lose it to any of the vultures who swarm around waiting for the seasonal boarders to move out." She pondered for a moment. "When the leaves change color should be a good time to turn back."

Laurie raised his brows and quickly tried to hide his surprise. That was considerably longer than he imagined she would want to stay. He would have to set aside time for sending correspondences to his employees, but the business was fortunately set up in such a way that his daily presence wasn't necessary.

"Grandfather has offered to have dinner ready for us when we are settled in."

"Oh, let's go tonight if it isn't too much trouble." Jo's eyes sparkled at the memory of the old man she loved so dearly and Laurie couldn't peel his eyes away from the soft glow her face held at the anticipation.

"I'm certain he would love that. Let's ask Marmee and your father if they'd join us, too."

"It's probably too late to send word for Meg."

"And Amy's in Europe."

"Again?" Jo frowned. "I can hardly keep up with where she's at and she stopped writing me back months ago."

"She's probably busy," Laurie mumbled.

"I can tell that's a lie, but I don't care enough to press you further. She's changed after getting Aunt March's money—and not for the better."

"Money doesn't change people, Jo. It expands what's already there."

"Well, her fortune has made it clear what was already there and I'm fine that she hasn't written back. It's freed up my own mind to not worry about her constantly."

Laurie sighed. It was painful seeing the agitation on Jo's face without being able to do anything about it. The youngest March sister had long been a weight heavy on Jo's conscience and time had not changed it in the way he hoped it would. He wanted to see peace between the two sisters, but he'd lived enough of his life to know that resolution seldom came in the places we most want it.

"At least the weather is fine for travel today."

"I won't say anything about how you're changing the subject for right now, but we can't avoid talking about Amy forever."

"She's created her life and I'm not a part of it. When I see her, I'll be cordial enough."

Laurie laughed, earning a scowl from Jo. He quickly silenced himself and looked out of the carriage.

Jo took in a deep breath and marveled at how clean the air was becoming. "I would like to remark on the fresh air, though I'm worried of being accused."

"Of what?"

"Of changing the subject again."

Another laugh escaped Laurie's lips and Jo found a smile tugging at the corners of her mouth. "The air is exceptionally fresh here. New York has too many horses in one place to ever smell this good."

Jo stretched in her seat. "That's right. Even the pastures of horses out this far don't have the same smell that we have being all crammed to-gether in such tight quarters."

"Could you see yourself returning home?" Laurie looked at Jo out of the corner of his eye.

"I am returning home now, aren't I?"

"That isn't what I meant, and you know it!"

"I don't know." Jo fiddled with the hem of her jacket. "I haven't been home since Beth—"

Laurie put his hand on her knee and gave it a gentle squeeze. "I'll be right by your side the entire time. If it's too painful for you to stay at Orchard House, you can stay with grandfather and I."

"Oh Teddy. I've been fretting over how I would be able to sleep tonight. Or to even relax back on the couch. I'm afraid of her slipping away from my memory, but the closer we get to home, the more scared I am of feeling her everywhere."

Laurie pulled Jo's head to his shoulder, know-ing she wouldn't resist the comfort, and also cer-tain she would never take the action on her own. He slowly petted her forehead, and the two rode on in comfortable silence until Orchard House came into view.

The grass was a shimmering green in the golden glow of the afternoon sun, and the bushes lining the walkway to the house provided an inviting pathway. A few flowers that survived spring blooms added pops of color to the picturesque landscape, and Laurie's heart swelled with joy at the sight.

He jumped out of the carriage first and put his hand out to help Jo alight. She took his hand, a beam of a smile on her lips, and stepped down to the ground.

Out of the carriage, she became acutely aware of their hands touching and hastily dropped his. She balled her hand up into a fist, trying to squeeze out the remnants of a feeling attempting to make itself known.

A glance at Laurie was too much.

Something stirred inside her at the sight of him standing there, in the golden beams of sunlight framing his face. Home. She genuinely felt like she was home, and it felt better than she could have imagined.

Before she could think too deeply about what it all meant, Marmee flew out of the front door, wiping her hands on her apron and crying out her name.

Jo forgot about everything else in the world as she disappeared into her mother's embrace.

6

"I t's sometimes difficult for me to admit when I'm wrong—because it happens so infrequently, you know, that I don't have experience with it—but I will say, being home has lifted a fog that I was unaware had settled over me."

Laurie walked silently next to Jo, not speaking for fear of breaking the spell she was under as she shed this fog and became more and more herself with each step. He stole a glance and noticed the rosiness in her cheeks, the light behind her eyes, and how the spring had returned to her feet.

A week at home had done her more good than anything he could have contrived on his own. His heart soared with a happiness he was unable to contain.

"Race you to the tree ahead?" he cried out, giving her no time to spare if she wanted to win.

She let out a frustrated mumble and picked up speed, hot on his heels. He turned to look back, and she took advantage of his split-second distraction to pull ahead. She touched the tree first and crumpled to the ground in laughter.

"You never could stay focused on the prize, Teddy. That's why I always beat you."

Laurie sat down next to her and grinned. "No, we simply have different views on what the prize is."

"Are you trying to say you let me win?" She arched her brows and pursed her lips.

His thoughts became muddled as he imagined what it would be like to kiss her. He was certain it would result in a slap across the face and swiftly shook his head. "I know better than to *let* you win at anything." He cleared his throat and attempted to sound normal, despite the emotion thick in his throat. "No, I would never dream of letting Jo March win anything. You beat me fair and square."

"Good. Now help me up. I seem to have gotten my shoe stuck in this root."

Laurie wiggled the foot free and helped her to her feet, closing his fist once their hands parted. Jo, once upright, ran ahead, calling over her shoulder. "Race you to the house!"

He shook his head and laughed as he trotted in her wake, knowing he could never hope to catch her now.

Sure enough, she was already in his grandfather's study, chatting away with him by the time he made his way to the house.

"We were about to send a search party for you!" His grandfather's eyes sparkled with mischief and a joy he seemed to only hold when Jo was in his presence. Laurie could understand the feeling.

"Once I knew I was beat, I took a more leisurely stroll home." He sat down in a chair opposite Jo and avoided looking her way.

"If it had been any opponent other than Jo here, I would ask why you didn't give it your all. I'm too far in my years to doubt she would win against anyone and anything she set her mind to." Laurie's grandfather sat back in his chair. "No, I should count myself lucky I've never had to compete with you in anything."

Jo grinned and stood up to walk around the study. She reached out to feel the spine of a few books before folding her hands behind her back. "I am certain you could beat me at a great deal of things." She raised her eyebrows and Laurie relaxed back in his chair at the comforting sight as his grandfather laughed in a gentle, easy way.

"No, my dear. You could have the world if you went after it."

Jo frowned, but made no mention of the struggles she was having with her uphill battle writing her novel. Laurie longed to comfort her in some way, but knew if he mentioned it before she did, she would be more than upset with him. Instead, he smiled at her comfortingly when she looked his way. She smiled back and hurriedly turned back to the books around her.

"Take any you like," grandfather said absent-mindedly as he returned to writing letters.

Jo, long past the false pleasantries of pretending as though she didn't actually want to borrow anything, selected a few titles from the shelves and tucked the books under her arm. "Thank you for these. I should head home now."

Laurie jumped up. "I can walk you."

"I'll hardly get lost—"

Grandfather, not looking up from his desk, cleared his throat. "Jo, let the young man walk you home. He most likely wants to speak to you privately, and isn't the best at saying things outright."

Jo smiled to herself, thinking of all the ways Laurie had perfectly expressed his feelings to her. She felt that same tinge of grief that had cropped up earlier and scowled.

Laurie noticed the look on her face and put his hands up in deference. "If you want to walk home alone, I'm hardly going to press the issue."

"No, I think I would like the company."

Laurie smiled at her, so open and friendly and warm that Jo had to look away. She followed his steps through the house and out to the front yard.

"This is nice. We haven't had a lot of time to talk alone since we've been here. I think that's one way that New York quite spoiled us."

Jo nodded thoughtfully. "Yes. You're right. It's a valuable thing to have a friend to confide in and the space to do so privately."

"So what's on your mind, Jo? I could see the wheels of your brain turning the entire time we were in the study."

"It's nothing new." Jo waved her hand dismissively. "I can't get the words right. Foolishly, I thought being home would fix everything, but I almost feel more lost than ever. It's as if all the memories I want to capture are swirling around too quickly for me to pluck any one of them out of the air and get them down onto paper."

Laurie fell in step next to her and looked around. He came to an abrupt stop, and Jo faltered when she realized she had gotten ahead of him. "What is it, Teddy?"

"I have an idea. Meet me out front tomorrow when the sun is rising."

Before Jo could ask him what mischief he was up to, Laurie had already begun the run back to his house. A bubble of laughter rose in Jo's throat, and she stood dumbfounded before she regained her senses and ran to her own house, figuring out how to prepare for a surprise adventure.

7

—·—

T RUE TO HIS WORD, Laurie stood at the front
door of Orchard House as the sun made its
first appearance for the day. Jo wiped the sleep
out of her eyes and bounded down the stairs to
usher him inside.

"What prank do you have in mind?"

Laurie beamed like a rascal filled with tomfool-
ery and grabbed her hand. "Let's go. We have a
full day planned and I want to get to all of it."

After a long trek through the woods, they came
to a familiar clearing, and the field beckoned to
Jo. She briskly wiped her eyes and turned her
back to Laurie. Out here, she could imagine her
sisters running around, causing a ruckus away
from anyone who could hear or scold them to be
more lady-like.

If she squinted her eyes and let her gaze soften, she could imagine Amy trailing after Meg, her golden hair shining in the sun, and her little legs struggling to keep up with her older sister's long, confident strides. Beth would be walking behind them, picking daisies and making crowns out of them as she meandered through the patches of flowers, taking the time to thoroughly enjoy every sight and scent she encountered.

With a few more steps, Jo's legs felt weak from all the walking and reminiscing, and she collapsed down into the field with a content exhalation. "What a day! Even though the walk was much longer than I remember it being, I needed this, my old fellow."

Laurie flopped down next to her, flat on his back, and stared up at the clouds passing overhead. "Me too. I didn't coerce you to come home just for yourself. I realize now that some part of me needed to be home, too."

"It's going to be sad returning to New York." Jo turned to look at him wistfully, pulling at his heart strings.

"Do we have to go back?"

"Yes. I can't stay here. I stayed up half the night and still couldn't find the words to start my story. If I can't even start it, how will I ever finish it?"

Laurie propped himself up on his elbow and a serene look settled across his face. "Why don't we talk about your sisters? Remember that old story Meg told repeatedly about how you burnt some of her hair off?"

"She tells it as if I burnt her entire head clear off her neck." Jo rolled her eyes and plucked out a piece of grass with a laugh. "That was the night we went to the dance, and I found a friend in you."

"Why not add that to the story?"

Jo chewed on that thought. "I suppose. It's hard to know what readers will find entertaining."

"Don't write to entertain them. Write what's in your heart."

Jo laid back and stared up at the sky. "It all seems like it happened so long ago, but it really wasn't."

"Very true. So much has happened since that first night." Laurie sighed and settled back again.

"Do you ever wonder what it would be like having your own group of daughters to raise?"

"No!" cried Jo. "Do you?"

"Absolutely. Getting to know the four of you and become a part of your family honorarily was the happiest time of my life. If I had a little girl, I'd name her Elizabeth to commemorate sweet Beth."

"You'd have to hope with all of your heart that she was half as good as my Beth."

Laurie smiled bittersweetly and rolled back onto his side. "I find it hard to believe that you wouldn't thrive as a mother with your own mob of girls swarming around you."

Jo scrunched up her face. "It's not for me. Marriage is restrictive, and I have too many dreams to tie myself down like that." She rose to her knees, too flustered to stay still. "No. Marriage is a prison I should wish never to find myself in."

"Oh, Jo. Marriage doesn't have to be restrictive. Be with someone who expands you and loves you for all of who you are." He sighed and studied her face. "Where do you get these ideas from?"

"Lots of places. What if Marmee wanted to be a famous writer? When would she have found the time?"

"I don't believe her dream was to be a writer, but I'll entertain this thought. If she wanted to be a writer, she would have made the time to write. Next question."

"Well, what about Meg? She's constantly changing diapers, washing said diapers, drying said diapers, only to pin those diapers back on her babies and start the entire cycle over again." Jo rose to her feet. "What kind of life is that?" she cried.

"I believe it's a life she loves. Haven't you seen the way her eyes light up when she talks about the twins? Just because their dreams differ from yours doesn't mean they're wrong."

"Alright. Then just because my dreams are different and don't include marriage, it doesn't mean *they're* wrong." Jo crossed her arms over her chest and looked down at Laurie.

He put his hand out and she pulled him up to his feet. "Okay, my old fellow. You're right. Writing is your dream, so let's see this through."

Jo opened her mouth, ready to argue. When the agreeable air of his statement reached her, she shut her mouth and linked her arm in his. "What do you have in mind?"

"What's bugging you most about your story?"

"I can't find the right opening words and I feel hopeless. It's like my brain is a wheel stuck in mud and no matter how hard I pry, I can't break it free."

"When we get back to the house, show me what you have and I'll see what I can help with."

Up in the garret, Jo bit her nails while Laurie read the best first page she had written so far. She knew it wasn't good, and she fretted over what he would say as his brows lifted and furrowed with no explanation. After what felt like an eternity, he set the page down and she rushed over to sit next to him.

"How bad is it?"

"Don't try to fancy it up. Simply write about all of us as we are—no better, no worse. Write about how content Meg is in a role that terrifies you, how Amy likes the finer things, and how Beth—well I'm not sure how to write about an angel in every sense of the word, but Jo, the character of Jo is a brilliant writer, and the fine fellow she's modeled after will figure it out." Laurie jumped to his feet, caught up in memories and the intoxicating allure of story crafting. "Write about the mishaps, the cozy evenings, the fine parties that made us pull our hair out, and about relationships formed for a lifetime. Put in things you think are a bore. Those are the things that might delight readers the most. Put it all in, Jo." Laurie circled the desk seven times during his impassioned speech while Jo sat back, dumbfounded and in awe.

He was right.

"Give me my pen." She put out her hand, and he obliged, slipping silently out of the room as she scribbled away with fervor.

'Christmas won't be Christmas without any presents,' grumbled Jo, lying on the rug.

'It's so dreadful to be poor!' sighed Meg, looking down at her old dress.

'*I don't think it's fair for some girls to have plenty of pretty things, and other girls nothing at all*" added *little Amy, with an injured sniff.*

'*We've got Father and Mother, and each other,' said Beth contentedly from her corner.*

Jo held up the paper to read it better and eyed the fire suspiciously, as if it might come to life, accustomed to receiving sacrifices from her. She pressed the paper to her heart and let forth a stream of tears that had been dammed up since her dearest Beth got sick for the final time. Tears that she thought had long-since dried up came pouring out and, mindful of the ink, she placed the paper delicately on the desk. Sitting back, she studied the words as a feeling of contentment washed over her.

8

— · —

"**H**OW IS NEW YORK?" Grandfather leaned back in his chair and tented his hands on the desk in front of him.

"Business is good. I've made a lot of new connections and feel pretty good about the future."

He raised his eyebrows and cleared his throat. "That isn't what I'm asking about, and I'm certain you know that."

"If I can speak frankly—"

"Of course you can. When do you ever speak in any other manner?"

"I am reaching the point where I fear I'll give up on Jo ever wanting to be with me. I could hold on to hope if we were together and simply postponing marriage, but we are no closer than we were before graduation."

Grandfather chuckled good naturedly. "The exact same? I find that hard to believe. In her letters to me, she always mentions you and it's always with fondness. You're an important person in her life."

"Not important enough to marry." Laurie swiped his hand down his face and groaned. "I hate how pitiful it makes me sound. If this were one of my friends, I'd suggest they move on with their life and quit acting like such a fool."

"Is that the advice you wish I'd give you?"

"No. I don't think so, anyway."

"What makes you feel the most pathetic?"

"If you share this with another soul, it would be most unforgiveable."

"Carry on. I hold a great many secrets you'd never be able to get out of me."

Laurie studied his grandfather's face and, despite the twinkle of glee in his eye, he deemed him a trustworthy confidant. "It's my greatest shame. I want Jo to be successful, but sometimes I wish she needed me enough, or rather, needed our money enough, that she would come running to me, begging for me to marry her."

Grandfather tapped his fingers together. "That is a predicament, but hardly the worst someone's ever wished for another person. It wouldn't be a marriage of love if she came to you in that way."

"I know. And I don't truly want that for her. I'd rather her be successful and happy without me rather than miserable and stuck with me against her choice."

"I'm certain Jo will find herself in a situation where she will be free to make a decision based on love and not out of desperation." Grandfather hid a smile, though his eyes betrayed him.

"How can you be sure?"

"I know her and, like I said, I have secrets that no one can ever unlock unless I allow them to. Trust me, boy. I know that whatever Ms. March chooses will be of her own accord."

"Okay," Laurie said apprehensively.

"Secrets aside, do you ever see her reducing herself to beg for anything? She commands the world. That's one of the things we all love about her. She's not one we have to worry about being forced into anything she doesn't want on at least some level."

"Quite true. Right now she's holed up in the garret writing her heart out. She's been up there for a few days now with no end to her creativity, and I'm glad of it."

"Has she had a tough time of it in the city?"

"I don't want to over speak because she keeps her problems close to her sleeve and doesn't like to air out what is going wrong." He leaned forward and bit his lip. "I will say, being home has done both of us a world of good."

"I'm glad to hear that. I knew being home would be good for the both of you and it worried me when she refused to come home for the past year—though it's understandable why."

"Concord is where she belongs, and, I daresay, where I do, too."

"Even traveling the world as you have, you would still choose to live here?"

"Absolutely," Laurie said with a conviction that surprised his grandfather.

"I hope that whatever the future holds, it will be filled with blessings for both of you. I wish I could live long enough to see both of you in the blissful state of happiness that I know will be waiting for you."

"Don't speak like that!" Laurie cried. "I'm certain you have many years ahead of you."

"That's the great tragedy of grandparents raising their grandchildren. We often don't live long enough to see the fruits of our labor." He smiled warmly at Laurie, the corners of his smile tinged with sadness. "I will leave you with this, though, my boy. What I've been able to see thus far will leave me with immeasurable pride and satisfaction."

Laurie's stomach knotted and he couldn't speak. His grandfather carried on with the conversation, mindful of the boy's feelings.

"I don't say any of this to stress you. I want you to know that your future is well-secured. I've been hard on you through the years and you've always been by my side. Those March girls changed our lives and I have you to thank for opening my heart to them. It made me see how strict I had been with you. But I needn't have worried. You've turned into a fine young man, despite all of my fretting and fussing."

"Thank you," Laurie said in a small voice. "I have a better life than I could have ever hoped for after my parents—" He bowed his head. "Just thank you."

"Now, go. We had the conversation I felt was important for us to have. I'm fine for right now and I want to see you enjoy the rest of your time here."

Laurie stood up and his grandfather clasped his shoulder. "I mean it when I say I'm proud of you."

Nodding softly, Laurie walked out of the study and up to his room, where he could let out the emotions that had built up during their discussion.

Up in his room, he could see Jo standing above her desk, looking down at the papers she had written, a peaceful smile on her face. His heart warmed at the sight, and he vowed to always help her find that smile.

9

— · —

A SOFT TAP AT the door made Jo jump in surprise. "Teddy!"

Jo's hair was even wilder and more unruly than normal from her secluded days spent writing, and Laurie reached out to tuck a stray lock behind her ear. "Would you be up for a picnic today?"

"Yes! After you read some of what I've wrote." She shoved a stack of papers in his hand and Laurie sat down to read through them better.

"You've been up here writing for a week." He pressed his hand to his forehead, worthy of any stage performance. "I've had to check in with Marmee to make sure you're fed and alive. This is the longest we've been apart since my college days. I daresay I was missing you." Laurie grinned mischievously. "I had no sight of you aside from some glimpses of your shadow as you paced the floor up here."

She smacked his arm and shook the stack of papers. "Read before I lose my nerve! We can talk afterwards!"

Fighting a laugh, Laurie settled into the chair and dove into Jo's work while she paced restlessly back and forth. If it had been his first time reading something of hers, the pacing would have been distracting. As it was, the frantic steps were a common background noise to reading for him and he got lost in the story.

Page after page piled up next to him as he worked his way through one of the most epic stories he had ever heard. A saga that spanned a year and felt like a lifetime ago. His heart ached at the memories on each page. He went from a soaring high, from reading about the moment he and Jo danced the night away, to the lowest of lows as Beth died all over again, her life immortalized forever on the pages of her sister's story. In between all of that, he saw a storyline develop.

Something he always hoped for, even if all of his advances should have made him lose hope.

With the last page read, Laurie sat back in the chair and contemplated how to form what he wanted to say. He had never gone about it the correct way, but he knew he had to try again. He could see something Jo was purposely turning away from. He stood up slowly and Jo stopped pacing, her face filled with expectant apprehension.

"How was it? It's only the beginning. I don't know how long it will take me to finish it." She wrung her hands together and Laurie hoped she couldn't hear the tremble in his heart as he stepped forward.

"Jo, I promise you we'd be good together. You think we wouldn't, but I've always known it. Deep inside, I know you can tell too." He held up the pages that were filled with her love for him. She wouldn't write about him in such a way if she didn't feel the same.

Jo stepped back, shaking her head the whole way. "No, Teddy. Give up on me. The story made you nostalgic and foolish. Don't read more into it than what's there."

"No, Jo. It's how I've always felt. These words just show me I'm not alone. I've always wanted you. Just you."

"Why me? I'm not going to amount to anything. I don't want to go around in all the social circles you do. They would think I was beneath you and would incessantly question why someone of your status would even look my way."

"It's not true, Jo. I don't even like those social circles. We don't have to do that. I would give up my whole life for you to be happy."

"That's the problem. I couldn't give up my life to make you happy. I would never ask you to give up your life. It's not right, Teddy."

"It's a life I want to give up. I'm not made for it at all. And I'd never ask you to give up your life—"

"You'd be fine with me writing all hours of the night?" Jo side-eyed him skeptically.

"Absolutely. I'd make sure the fire stayed burning."

"I doubt that. You'd be sick of it after a week. And what about children? I don't know if I want children. I wouldn't be a good mother, that's for sure." Jo threw her hands up and began walking rapidly in circles, her voice rising and falling with each turn. "Marmee seems to have figured it all out and created a brilliant life for all of us despite anything going on, but I don't have that same cleverness. What about that hard year when father was away for the war? She was incredible and rose to the occasion. If we had children, I'd ruin them in everyday, ordinary occasions. They'd turn out wicked and unloved because all I'd do is neglect them or get angry with them."

At this, Laurie soothingly placed his hands on Jo's shoulders and looked her square in the eye. "That's a lie. Jo, I know you and you are all things good. You would be the best mother and make sure those children were never lacking for love." He rubbed her shoulders briskly and softened his face. "Jo, it's in your nature to love fiercely. I wish you could see yourself the way I see you."

"You're wrong."

"No, I'm not. I've never been more right about anything. Why won't you marry me, Jo? We'd be happier than either of us can even imagine right now."

"I'm not taken to flights of fancy like you. I see things for how they are."

"Ah yes, Jo March, the realist with no imagination. That's precisely what you are." He handed her the stack of papers in his hand. "Such admirable qualities in a writer."

"Teddy, stop. This wouldn't be good. You'd hate me and resent me."

"I sometimes already do."

"That's good to know. I'll leave you alone."

"That isn't what I meant. I just get so frustrated with you."

"Because I won't match what you want. I can't conform to your standards."

"Jo!" Laurie cried. "I don't want you to change. I want you to open yourself up. Be more of yourself!"

Jo shook her head. "No. Head home, Teddy. I'm tired and need to clear my mind before I can find sleep."

"I'd rather be miserable waiting for you to love me than miserable with someone else. Goodnight Jo."

Laurie hung his head as he walked out of the March house and Jo felt a twinge of anguish in her heart. She couldn't stand how he was so ignorant to how a union between the two of them would ruin his life.

10

J O SKIPPED DOWN THE stairs, hoping to find Marmee alone and free to talk. Her mind was racing with Laurie's latest proposal and she couldn't sit still after he left.

"Marmee?" She turned into the living room and halted abruptly when she saw who was sitting on the couch.

"I believe Marmee said she'd be back home in a half hour and it has been close to that." Amy stood up and made her way over.

"I didn't know you'd be home."

Amy looked her sister up and down. "I didn't know you would be here either. I suppose this results from not writing to each other enough."

"I wrote you plenty, but it became tiresome when I never received a reply."

Amy shrugged and ran her hand along the arm of the couch. "I suppose time went by more quickly than I figured it would. I'm home now, dear sister, at least for now. We shall catch up and have a jolly good time."

Jo, longing for the old days, wrapped her arms around her sister and wished the two of them were closer. "I'm glad to see you, Amy. It really has been too long. How was Europe?"

"Oh, you know. It gets a little much some-times—oh, who am I kidding? It's not too much, but it is nice coming home every once in a while for some quiet and where no one expects any-thing of me."

"Have you moved into Aunt March's—I mean, your house—yet?"

"No. I'm having some extensive renovations done. I can't believe I thought it was such a grand house when I was a girl. In the daylight of my adulthood, it's clear that much of it is outdated and in need of updating." She waved her hand dismissively in the air, and Jo tried to keep up.

"Ah, I see."

"How has New York been? I don't blame you for leaving during the summer. I hear it gets dreadfully hot."

"It was Teddy's idea to leave for home."

"Ah, dear Laurie. He ran out of here in a flash when I was arriving. What was that about?"

Jo groaned and dropped her head in her hands. She wrestled with whether or not her sister would be a trusted confidant, but didn't have to consider it for long when Marmee burst through the door.

"Girls! I'm glad you're together. I ran into Mr. Laurence on the way home."

Here, Jo held her breath, which Amy noticed and met with a reproachful brow raise.

"He's asked us all to dinner tomorrow night. I mentioned Amy had just arrived home, and he thought it would be a wonderful idea to invite Meg and John to dine with all of us. I told him yes."

"Oh, of course Marmee!" Amy cried.

"Jo, why do you look so dismal over this news?"

Amy leaned forward and whispered with an exaggerated air. "I do believe our Jo had a spat with Laurie. She was just about to tell me everything."

Jo glowered at her sister, but resigned herself to tell both women what had happened. As much as she didn't want Amy's judgment, it might be nice to have both of their opinions on what she should have done. She looked back and forth between both of their willing faces and took a deep breath.

"He proposed to me. Again."

"How many times has he proposed?" Amy was absolutely flabbergasted at this news, while Marmee nodded thoughtfully and didn't say anything.

"Twice?"

"Jo!" Amy cried. "Why would you turn him down twice?"

"We're better as friends," Jo said sheepishly.

Marmee, still quiet, looked back and forth between both daughters. Jo silently begged for her mother to say something. Anything. She needed her warm wisdom to pacify her fears.

After what felt like an eternity to Jo's nerves, Marmee sat forward and cleared her throat. "Jo, my dear Jo, I want you to do what makes you most happy. Do you love him?"

"I don't know. I really haven't thought of him in that way."

"Are there any men that you have thought of in that way?"

"Not really. I've been so wrapped up in writing, and love is the last thing on my mind."

"Really? I find that hard to believe. I've had to turn down at least five potential suitors a week." Amy shrugged when Marmee shot her a severe look. "It's true. I thought everyone around our age had to fight back the men. Well, I do suppose I am a few years younger."

"I think that's enough from you, Amy." Marmee's voice left no room for disagreement, and Amy sat back on the couch with a pout.

"I'm not even sure I know what love is," Jo said wistfully. "At least I know that the friendship we have right now is real. Marrying him would ruin that, and I can't bear the thought."

"Your father and I have a deep friendship that has only strengthened over the years as husband and wife."

"Yes, but that is the two of you. I could hardly hope to live up to such high standards."

Marmee stood up to leave the room and patted Jo's knee. "My dear, there are no high standards anyone is holding anyone else to, except those you put upon yourself."

She exited the room and Amy leaned forward in her seat. "I believe it's healthy to hold ourselves to high standards. If you don't believe you're worthy of Laurie, then you aren't." Amy pursed her lips and turned up her chin. "Our dear Laurie deserves someone who truly loves him and is worthy of him."

Jo picked at the cushion sitting next to her until a thread poked out. She knew Amy was right. She was hardly worthy of someone like Laurie and she was thankful she turned him down, if only for his sake. As for herself, she couldn't press down the gnawing feeling that she was missing something she desperately needed in her life.

11

MEG HANDED JO A bowl of sliced apples and Jo began working the cinnamon and sugar into it. She stopped to sniff the mixture and closed her eyes at the thought of how good it would taste that evening after dinner at the Laurence's.

"What's on your mind?"

"What?" Jo looked over at her eldest sister in shock. "I didn't say anything was wrong."

"No, but you never stop to smell things and you never bake without complaining about something. What's going on?"

Jo shrugged and returned to stirring. "I wouldn't say anything's wrong."

"Fess up. I know you and we don't have a lot of time without anyone here. John has the babies over visiting Mr. Laurence, and that will only last until they're ready for their nap. Marmee and Amy will be back from the store any time now and Father is only going to sit outside for so long before he's ready to come back in." She gave Jo a stern look that made her stand taller. "Out with it."

"Do you resent John for how much you've had to give up and how hard your life is?"

"I'd hardly say I have a difficult life."

"But you're so cross with everyone more now than you've ever been."

Meg stared at her sister and Jo felt like crawling under the table. Her words came out more accusatory than she meant, and she would do anything to begin again.

"I'm overwhelmed, Jo. It happens to all of us, but I wouldn't trade this life for anything. Being overwhelmed doesn't mean I'm not myself, it simply means I'm overwhelmed."

"But what about all of your dreams?"

"John and I work together. We have a small farm that takes care of most of our needs. We have beautiful children I could've only ever dreamed of. I don't want for anything. My life is a good life."

"I didn't mean to imply it's not." Jo's cheeks reddened. "I don't see how I could ever have that, though." She winced at how her voice tightened and betrayed her.

"Could my fierce and independent Jo be considering marriage?" Meg teased just enough to bother Jo without making her run and Jo, fully aware of this finessing, scowled at her sister.

"No." She dug the toe of her shoe into the worn out rug on the kitchen floor. "Well, I don't know. Right now, I feel more conflicted and unsure of myself than ever before, but I did say no."

"Jo!" Meg cried. "Who asked you?"

"Teddy, of course."

"Jo!" Meg seemed to be able to say no other words.

"Don't yell at me!"

"Jo!"

"Well! I wasn't going to throw my life away and be tied to some man."

"Seriously, Jo. You're as tied to that boy as you possibly could be without marrying him. Don't you love him?"

"I thought I didn't. I thought he was just a brother to me, but the more I go through life, the more I realize what love truly is, I think I do in fact love him." She laid her elbows on the counter and hung her head.

"Then go to him. Quit wasting your time here. Goodness knows Laurie only went to New York to be near you."

"That's not true, Meg. His grandfather sent him there on business—"

"Yes, a convenient excuse." Meg crossed her arms over her chest and looked up at her younger sister. "He did it so Laurie could have a sensible reason for being there. Once Laurie came back from Europe, all he talked about was wanting to stay in Concord. Why do you think that changed?"

Jo shrugged apprehensively.

"You! Jo, he went to New York for you."

"No, that can't be true." She backed away from the counter she had been leaning against and thought about every all-to-convenient situation she had found herself in, especially regarding Teddy.

The way they'd always run into each other. They both found excuses to see each other every single day of the last year. It hadn't stood out as strange since that was how it was at home, but in a big city like New York, it was out of the ordinary to see the same person day after day without living with them.

She raised her hand to her mouth and reached out for the counter to steady herself with her other hand. "Meg. I've made a big mistake. I've rejected him too many times and the last time was probably my last chance to say yes." She ran her hand through her hair. "Oh, Meg! Why do I do this to myself?"

Meg rushed over to hug her sister. "No, Jo. I doubt he'd ever give up on you. If the love you two have is true, and I believe with all my heart it is, he'll be thrilled to hear you say you know how you feel."

"I don't know how I feel. That's most of the problem. What if I say I love him and I find out that he's simply like a brother to me and I ruin both of our lives?"

"Oh, Jo. I don't have a suitable answer for you. I wish I did. With John, I just knew."

"You had no doubt?"

Meg scrunched up her face. "Okay, maybe a little. I was so young and unsure of everything. But when Aunt March told me I couldn't marry him or I'd lose my inheritance, I knew in that moment what my heart wanted." Meg's face hardened into resolve as she relived the moment. "I imagined myself holed up in that big old house with money, but no love, and then I imagined John's face looking at me lovingly and I was no longer scared."

"I didn't say I was scared!" Jo cried.

"Hopefully that remark doesn't actually mean you missed the entire point of my speech." Meg shook her head and laughed. "Oh, Jo. You can be so impossible sometimes."

"No, no. I heard you." Jo slumped down into one of the kitchen chairs, grimacing as the hard wood met her spine roughly with the careless movement. "I've never had to make such a hard decision. Or at least, any time I've been in this position, I ignore the decision."

"Talk to him. Don't argue with him. Truly sit down and talk to him about your fears and concerns and see what he has to say."

"We have the dinner that all of us will be at. I can't talk to him there."

"No, but you can talk to him afterwards. Ask him on a walk and get him to yourself."

Jo wouldn't have admitted, even under torture, how hard her stomach flopped at the idea of walking alone with him. It was something she had done countless times, but this time it felt more intimate, and she wasn't sure she could do it.

12

—·—

"AH, THE BABIES LOOK refreshed and mischievously playful after their nap." Mr. Laurence beamed with pride and put his arms out for John to hand him Daisy, while Meg sat down next to him with the plump, rosy-cheeked little boy, Demi, after the two parents had left at the end of dinner to grab the babies who were just rousing from their sleep in another room.

With the babbling girl on his lap, Mr. Laurence looked around at the group assembled around his table. "Thank you all for indulging an old man and coming over for dinner. It's been a delightful evening."

"Of course! We're always happy to dine with you and have you over to our house." Marmee grinned back at him and the two shared a look of deep reverence, born over years of being close friends and neighbors.

"I will always be grateful for my young Laurie here. He befriended you girls, despite my wishes to keep him more reined in. I admit I was in the wrong during those early years. The companionship you Marches have given the two of us lonely men has been something we can never repay."

"Oh, nonsense. Don't talk of repayment, Mr. Laurence. It is I who can never repay you. The help and friendship you gave my little women during that long cold year when I was at war was something I can never return to you." Father choked over his words. "And what you've done since then, especially in the wake of all the difficulty that came after, was something no mortal could ever hope to recompense you for."

He couldn't speak of Beth's name without tearing up, but no one sitting around the table had any doubt about what difficulty he meant. They all bowed their heads and sat silently as thoughts of their dear, sweet Beth flooded their minds.

Demi giggled and clapped his hands together, drawing everyone up out of their memories. "Hey there, little Demi," Meg whispered into his ear and everyone watched with smiles on their faces as he cooed and looked around the room at all the people who loved him most dearly.

"Grandchildren are certainly the best creatures to come out of this wretched world." Grandfather patted Daisy's head. "As much as I love these two as if they were my own, I must admit I get impatient for Laurie to bring news of a wife so I might see a great-grandchild in my lifetime."

Laurie stole a glance at Jo, who had been studiously avoiding him all evening for fear of what she would say. She spent the afternoon fretting over their impending talk and how she would get him alone with everyone in town. At certain points during dinner, she felt as if she would burst into tears and the sensation had her trembling with nerves.

One such thing that felt like it would send her over the edge was the look on Laurie's face as the two made eye contact. She glanced away and pretended as if her fork were the most interesting item she had ever seen in her life.

Amy cleared her throat and flashed everyone a smile that dazzled the room before landing her affections on Laurie. "I believe he'll find someone most worthy of his regard. He is an easy man to love and I'm sure he has no trouble in that department, even if he's bashful about it to all of us." She gave a coquettish look to Laurie, who blushed at the boldness of her words. "Since none of those prospects are currently here, might I ask you for an after-dinner stroll around the gardens? I do have so much to tell you about Europe."

Laurie's eyes flicked back over to Jo, who had all of her attention on Demi, and turned back to Amy with a small smile. "That sounds lovely, Amy. We do have a lot to catch up on."

Only Marmee and Meg noticed the increased redness on Jo's cheeks before she excused herself. "Dinner was lovely." She kissed grandfather on the cheek. "I must get back to my story. I'm at a pivotal part and in desperate need to get these words out of my head."

He stood up and grabbed her by the shoulders before embracing her tightly. "I'll see you to the door myself."

As they walked through the house, Grandfather smiled sweetly at her and her heart warmed. He turned to face her and something in the way he held the corners of his mouth made heart falter. "My dearest girl, I fear I'm not long for this world," he whispered so only she could hear.

"No!" Jo cried quietly. "I won't let you speak in such a manner. Surely you have years and years ahead of you."

He shrugged, and his mouth curled up into a sad smile. "It's true. This day will come for all of us. I want you to know that when I'm gone, I've made arrangements that will see you through the rest of your life." He closed his eyes tightly before opening them back up to reveal a glistening that made Jo shift on her feet. "I've always believed you and my grandson would marry, but that will be left up to fate and time, time that I unfortunately do not have enough of. I love your whole family, but it is you that I most see as a kindred spirit and feel as if you are already truly my family.

If you married Laurie, you would never want for anything in your life. But as that isn't happening the way I thought it would when he first told me about you, I wanted to make sure that you are provided for no matter what you choose in life. I won't burden you with details now, my dear, but please know that anything I bestow to you is of my own will and not for any ulterior motives other than to make sure someone I care about has the life I believe she deserves."

By the end of his words, Mr. Laurence's breathing became a bit of a struggle. Jo linked her arm with his and guided him over to a chair in the fo yer. "Sit here a moment and catch your breath."

"Thank you, dear. I don't want the others to see me like this." He looked up at Jo with a grateful smile and she patted his shoulder lovingly.

When he felt strong again after a brief rest, she helped him to his feet and watched as he made his way back to the dining room.

His words echoed in her mind as she walked home. He was a kind, old gentleman who had improved her life in so many ways. Her heart ached at the thought he wouldn't live to see

a great-grandchild from Laurie and she enter-
tained the thought that a twinge of the pain
might perhaps be rooted in her longing for the
same thing.

Up in the garret, she wrestled with the mul-
titude of present problems swirling in her head
as she attempted to recall the past in a way that
did justice to all of her sisters. Her mind reeled
with conversations before, during, and after dinner, and she wasn't sure how to drown them out
enough to allow in old memories of putting on
plays and dressing up with the ridiculous cos-
tumes they all came up with.

She looked out the window, trying to draw inspiration from the setting sun, but her eyes land-
ed on Laurie and Amy walking around the Laurence's garden. Their arms were linked, and the
two threw their heads back in laughter. Whether
or not they were talking about her, she couldn't
let herself care. It hurt either way to know Amy
was out having fun with Laurie while Jo sat at
home with unspoken words on her tongue, trying
her best not to cry.

13

—·—

"Jo! Aren't you coming down for breakfast?" Amy's voice cut through Jo's restless dreams and her eyes snapped open.

She would have rather woken up in her room in Ms. Springer's boarding house. Groaning, she pulled the covers up over her face. Amy sat on the edge of her bed, much too excited to let her sleep any longer.

Once she was certain her sister wouldn't leave unless she talked first, Jo ripped the blanket away from her and sat up. "What is it?"

"What?" asked Amy modestly.

"Why are you waking me up? I was up all night writing and I needed more sleep." She fittingly left out the part that she *attempted* to write all evening, but the words wouldn't come to her with the image of Amy and Laurie walking happily hand-in-hand burned into her mind.

"I spoke with Laurie last night." Amy looked at Jo to assess her reaction. "After dinner, when we walked."

Jo raised her eyebrows. "I hope you didn't talk to him about what we talked about?"

"Oh, heavens no! He was in such great spirits walking around with me as his company that I would never dream of bringing him down like that."

Jo winced at the slight and impatiently waited for Amy to finish whatever she came in to tell her.

"The walk was wonderful. Laurie is really everything a perfect gentleman should be, and I found myself admitting that in my heart, I know I'm in love with him."

"Amy!" cried Jo.

"What? I'm sorry Jo, but it isn't my fault you couldn't tell him how you feel and I could. The two of you have had more opportunities than any two people I've ever met and it's time someone spoke up."

"So what does this mean? The two of you are getting married now?"

"I don't know what our future holds, but I can't wait to get there." Amy looked out the window, over towards the Laurence house and a soft smile played on her lips.

"Of all the cruel things you've done to me, this one really beats all."

"Jo, we're getting older and it isn't fair of you to waste the poor boy's life that way." Amy shrugged and ran her hand across the windowsill, inspecting her finger afterwards. "I've done both of you a favor."

"Please get out of my room. I'm certain—no, not certain—I'm *hopeful* you aren't as wicked as you're making yourself out to be right now."

"Jo—"

"Out!" Jo cried.

Jo slumped back onto her bed and stifled a sob. Amy and Laurie? She couldn't bear the thought. Her mind raced over all the memories she had recently dredged up, trying to make sense of this connection, and she fell short. It simply didn't make sense.

A vision of their merry faces as they strolled through the gardens flashed in her mind and she shut her eyes against the pain of the sight. She apparently had missed something between the two of them and now she would have to live as Laurie's sister-in-law.

"Amy knew how I felt. Now this feels like betrayal."

"Did she truly know how you felt? When we talked, you were unsure of your feelings."

"No, I suppose not, but it still seems awfully underhanded to take him before I even had the option to decide."

"Amy does have a way of deciding she wants something and going after it with the intent of getting it." Marmee smiled affectionately at Jo. "Sometimes that benefits all of us and sometimes it only benefits herself."

Jo buried her head in her hands. "Marmee. I don't know what to do."

"Have you decided if you truly love him? Let yourself be sad either way, but it is wise of you to understand if it's worth hanging onto any sliver of hope that your darling sister is simply being fickle."

"I do love him. I didn't realize it because I thought that what we had was enough, but the thought of losing him—if you could call it losing him—is too much, Marmee."

Marmee pulled her close to her chest and stroked Jo's chestnut hair softly. "There, there. It can be hard to see what we have until it's threatened. To some, that may not be their definition of love, but I, too, have experienced a similar situation."

Jo looked up at her with tear-soaked cheeks. "You have?"

Marmee smiled softly and nodded. "Yes. I wasn't sure I wanted children. I was worried about my temper getting in the way and I thought I'd be unfit to mother."

"No! You are the best mother in the world!" Jo cried.

Marmee patted her head. "I wasn't sure of my ability at all and dreaded the day my first baby was born. She was adorable, of course, but something in my heart stayed closed off to her. Hannah was a big help during this time. She made sure I fed the baby and made sure I took care of myself as well."

Marmee sighed, her breath shaky with emotion. "The winter after Meg was born, she caught a cold and developed a worse case of croup than any I'd ever heard and any I've heard since." She closed her eyes against the painful memory. "I sat outside with her, night after night, begging for her life to be spared. I prayed with all my might that her lungs would keep working and that her breathing would clear up."

She opened her eyes again, and a bittersweet look fell across her face. "I should have known before that moment that I loved her with a ferocious depth not easily duplicated, but I didn't. I realized it once she almost slipped away from me. At that moment, I decided to open myself up to love. Life is precious, and I didn't want to waste a moment being angry with myself for not loving all four of you girls with my entire heart."

Jo rested her chin on Marmee's shoulder. "If it helps, I've never felt a single second of a single day that you didn't love us with every fiber of your being."

Marmee kissed her cheek. "I hope this all works out for the best for all three of you. It's a terrible predicament and sometimes I wish all four of you were little girls again, bemoaning the weather instead of these adult problems that seem never ending."

"Me too. Life seemed so hard and difficult back then, but it also felt so full of hope and magic. What I wouldn't trade to go back to the days where we traipsed through the fields and made up the silliest characters and stories."

"Life will have that magic for you again soon. I'm sure of it." Marmee pulled Jo close to her and Jo leaned hard against the support of her doting mother, thankful for what she did have, even if what she didn't have was leaving a gaping wound in her heart that felt as though it would never heal.

14

A MY CAME IN THE door like a tornado, her cheeks flushed and her eyes shining. She grinned at Jo as she passed her hat off to her. Jo took the hat, looked down at it with a befuddled face, and tossed it unceremoniously onto the couch.

With a huff, Amy retrieved the hat and scowled at Jo. "This cost a lot of money. I'll have you know!"

"Then don't hand it off to me. I thought it was simply an ordinary hat from your old collection."

Amy narrowed her eyes and held the hat close to her heart. "As if I would wear anything from then."

"If it's something still useful and enjoyable, why get something new?"

"The thrill of it, for one." A devilish grin spread across her face that made Jo's stomach lurch. "I see what I want and I go for it."

Jo repressed an eye roll and made for the kitchen. Amy skipped to catch up with her.

"Aren't you curious about my day with Laurie?"

"Not particularly."

Jo tried her absolute hardest to not find joy in how flustered her sister became at her flippant disinterest. She hid a smile as she got to work on a pair of socks she had been darning to help her work out a twist in her book that wasn't turning out in an entertaining enough way. Her thoughts strayed to how nice it would be to have Laurie to bounce ideas off of. She would ask him how he remembered it and then work it together with how she had stored the memory. Together they would come up with something accurate and interesting.

But she couldn't do that.

Instead, she was forced to share a room with Amy, who seemed bursting to tell her something. Jo focused painstakingly as she worked her knitting needles, taking care to never look up. Amy sat on the couch across from her, sighing every so often, and Jo found immense pleasure in her discomposure until it began imposing on her own peace of mind.

"What is it?"

Amy sat forward, her elbows on her knees, and took in a deep breath to prepare herself for the tale she was about to tell. "Laurie and I spoke about Europe and he suggested we take a trip together. Isn't that delightful?" She clapped her hands together and looked at Jo for her response.

"Seriously Amy?"

"I thought you'd be happy for us?" Amy fiddled with the hat in her lap and tucked a silk flower back in that she accidentally pulled out.

"I am happy, but I can be sad at the same time, too."

"Jo, I mean this as a caring sister—you can't keep lamenting over what you rejected. It's not Laurie's fault he wants to move on and not be reminded of a constant source of rejection.

Jo bit back all the words she wanted to say and merely nodded before returning to her work.

Once she no longer felt the need to say a scathing response, she took a steadying breath. "Amy, I am happy for you. Teddy does deserve the world and if that's with you, then I shall be the model older sister and love both of you with all my heart."

Amy sat back with a self-satisfied air and spoke when the front door flew open, startling both women out of their seats.

"It's grandfather." Laurie gasped for air. "He's not responding." He shook his head. "The doctor's there." His next few words sounded as if someone put a vise on his throat. "He said he's gone." Laurie's face crumpled into a look of grief that burned into Jo's memory with a resolute permanence.

At this news, Jo felt as if the world around her was suddenly underwater. She saw her feet making their way over to Laurie, fighting to take each step, as if she couldn't increase their speed as they walked through an imagined mud. Every motion was slowed down and over-exaggerated and driving her crazy. He looked at her with a sadness that she longed to comfort and soothe and silently cursed her body for not cooperating.

Out of the corner of her eye, Jo saw movement fly by at a speed that seemed dizzying. It took a second to register in her mind that it was Amy, who clearly had better control of her faculties, and made it to him first.

Jo's steps halted as she watched her sister wrap her arms around Laurie's neck, sobbing. Marmee came running from the kitchen, wiping her hands on her apron before putting her arms around Amy and Laurie, tears freely falling from her face as soon as she realized what was wrong. Marmee reached out her hand to include Jo in the clumsy group hug and at that moment, Jo's feet dislodged themselves from the imaginary mud and she flew out the door, the hinges creaking behind her as it slammed closed.

She didn't hear the bang for she was already to her favorite tree she usually enjoyed the solace of. In this moment, the silence felt like a pressure around her head. She stretched her jaw to relieve the crushing feeling, only to find no relief.

She wilted against the tree, its sturdy trunk keeping her from falling into the earth. From her isolated place of bereavement, she could see the peaks of the Laurence house and she couldn't imagine that Mr. Laurence wasn't currently sitting at his desk, writing letters, and calling for Laurie to come in and discuss something to do with their businesses.

She spent hours like this while the world went through its normal motions. The sun set, the stars came out, and she sat, motionless as the tree, until she drifted off into a fitful sleep.

She awoke when the sun lit up the sky and birds came out to greet the new day. Their chirps sounded offensive and ill-mannered, as if the natural kingdom did not receive word of the great loss the world had experienced only a day before.

Sometime during the night, someone had found her and draped a blanket around her. A small basket of food had been left for her and she nibbled its contents, more out of a necessity for strength. Her appetite was gone and the bread could have been made of mud for as bland as it tasted to her, it brought her no comfort.

She leaned back against the tree trunk, working a tight spot in her shoulder as she focused on a figure coming towards her in the distance.

John rushed over, carrying an envelope and waving her down. "Your father told me I could find you out here." He stooped against the tree to catch his breath while Jo opened the envelope and read its contents.

"Is this true?" she asked after several moments of staring at the words on the page

"All of it," John said breathlessly as he bobbed his head vigorously. "It was one of his last wishes and he made sure I'd be the one to tell you first, so you had time to absorb the information before the more formal reading of his will."

"That old sweetheart knew me all too well. I can't believe any of this."

She pressed the letter to her heart and sent a thank you heavenward, where she was certain the kindest old gentleman had arrived and taken up residence.

15

"IT STILL SEEMS SO surreal. His letter said Teddy was informed as well. I don't know how that will work, but I'm glad that I'll have someone living with me that I trust so wholeheartedly, even if it's rough right now." Jo's face fell as the reality of the current situation hit her. "Although, if he does marry Amy and she is living there, too, how will that work?"

Marmee held Jo tightly against her as they faced the warmth of the fire lighting up the otherwise dark room. "Amy has Aunt March's house, so I don't believe she would want to stay at the Laurence house. Actually, do we call it the Laurence house now that it's yours?"

"I don't know. I don't know how to respond to any of it. He left me the house I've loved since I was a child and enough money to never have to worry about a thing in my life ever again."

"Did he say what he was leaving Laurie?"

Jo pulled out the letter that she had kept close to her since receiving it and read aloud a few lines to Marmee. "It sounds like he's inheriting all of the businesses and a substantial amount of money, along with the apartment in New York."

"I'm glad that both of you will be well taken care of. I believe in your book and all of your dreams, so don't take this as criticism in that area, but it brings father and I immense relief that all three of our beautiful girls will be okay for the remainder of their days. Though, we do still worry about the future for Meg and John—"

"Oh, don't worry, Marmee!" Jo cried. "I shall have more money than I'll know what to do with. If something were to happen to Meg or John, I will be certain that the other never need want for anything."

Jo sat silently for long enough that Marmee gently asked her what was going through her mind.

"I can't possibly begin to imagine why Mr. Laurence would leave me the house. It's not as if I did anything to deserve it. He might not have been aware that I rejected Teddy, but he certainly knew I had never said yes if I had been asked."

"Mr. Laurence spoke to your father and I about the inheritance." She put her hand up to silence Jo when the statement was met with a sudden jolt. "We all wanted the best for the two of you and he figured that by leaving you the house, you would be free to marry for love and never out of desperation."

"But what if I don't marry Teddy? It's already out of my future and doesn't look as if it will change."

"He thought of that and nothing about his gift was an intimidation to force you into anything you didn't want. His greatest wish was that you would be a woman of means who had freedom. He knew how much it bothered Meg when those awful girls gossiped that you were all friends with Laurie for his money. This way, whoever you marry, there will be no talk of marrying for money." Marmee's eyes danced with memories. "He said that even though he was an old-fashioned man whose time in the world was long-past, he believed your views on how the world was unfair for women. He said he could do this small part to give you a small portion of what you deserve."

"Oh, but it's a greater portion than I would ever consider myself deserving of!" cried Jo.

Marmee smoothed back Jo's hair and kissed her forehead. "My dear girl, you deserve the world. Never forget that."

"Still, it seems like too big of a gift."

"Truly, though, the gift isn't the house. He gave you the gift of freedom and a clear conscience. How honest it will be if you do marry, knowing that whoever it is was someone you chose based on love?"

"It seems all too tragic that this is all set up so perfectly just when I've lost Laurie forever. My heart cannot bear the grief. I've lost two such important people in my life in a matter of days."

Marmee stroked Jo's back and sighed. "Whether it's Laurie or not, I have faith you'll find the person who completes you. You're someone who loves deeply and fiercely, and I know you'll find someone worthy of that love."

Jo bit her lip and thought of the one person who fit all of what Marmee said. She silently chastised herself for letting Laurie slip through her fingers.

That night, she drifted off to sleep imaging herself in the big house, covered in jewels she didn't want, with no one by her side. The lonely ache didn't leave her as she woke up to face the day of Mr. Laurence's funeral.

16

—— ◆ ——

J O WRAPPED HER SHAWL about her tightly as she followed between Marmee and Meg to the house to grab their food for a dinner the town was having in honor of Mr. Laurence's death after the funeral ended. She tensed her arms to try and remove the ache from them that she had felt the entire funeral. Laurie had sat in the front row, his head bowed the entire time, with Amy by his side, doting on him, offering him tissues, and whispering small words of comfort in his ear.

All the while, Jo's arms longed to be the ones to comfort him. Instead, she sat behind the two of them and mourned alone as she felt the gravity of never again seeing someone who was like her own grandfather.

The burial behind the house in the small family plot was even harder. Jo hung near the back by Marmee and father and watched as Mr. Laurence was lowered into the ground in his final resting place. She looked around at the enormous house and the weight of everything he had ever done for her family came crashing out of her eyes in waves of tears she thought would never stop.

Laurie stayed near his grandfather's coffin, his head bowed, and once again, Amy by his side, offering to talk to anyone who came up to him with condolences. In that moment, Jo was thankful for her sister and her ability to talk to anyone so easily and leave them feeling the better for talking to her. Laurie certainly appreciated it as well.

Back at Orchard House, Marmee softly doled out orders to her two oldest grief-stricken daughters to keep them on task as the town gathered nearby. Meg and Jo finished up everything with their mother and sat down to breathe for a moment before facing the crowd.

"How are you doing, Jo?" Meg looked at her with such a tender motherly look that Jo had to bite the corner of her cheek to stop herself from crying.

"Miserable. I can't fathom how awful Teddy is feeling, and I can't be there to comfort him."

"Why can't you?"

"Amy—it's been weird between the three of us."

"You can be there for your oldest and dearest friend. Surely even Amy would see the merit in that."

"She doesn't leave his side. How can I?"

Meg pointed her chin towards the window. "Amy's out talking to Mr. Penniwick and I saw Laurie head into the house by himself when we were walking home."

"Oh, I might have been doing my best to avoid looking in their direction. I didn't notice."

"Go to him, Jo. He needs his best friend."

Jo ran through the house, calling out for Laurie and getting worried with every second she didn't hear an answer to her calls. The servants had all attended the funeral and then had been sent away for a break by Laurie afterwards. The house felt strange and cold with no one bustling about or keeping the fires burning. It was disorienting running through each hall as the cloths hadn't been removed from the mirrors and she hoped she would find Laurie soon.

Most of the doors were closed, but a small crack of light shone through the library door. Jo slipped inside, hoping this was where she would find who she was looking for. She rushed over when she saw her friend sitting on the floor, tears staining his cheeks.

"Don't mind me, Jo. I thought I'd spend some time in here alone. I can still smell grandfather and keep expecting him to walk through the door to ask me what I'm doing sitting down here."

"It does seem as if he'll walk through the doors at any moment." Jo walked over and lit a fire in the hearth, rubbing the chill out of her arms.

"When will you be heading back to Ms. Springer's?"

"I can't go back. I belong here in Concord. This is my home."

"I hope grandfather's will isn't forcing you to stay here—"

"No!" Jo cried. "I've already made up my mind. I talked to Marmee days ago about moving back into the house." Jo looked around the room with an uneasy smile. "I suppose that conversation doesn't matter now that I have my own home."

"I'll be out of here as soon as I can pack up my things."

"Why?"

"I would never want to be in your way."

"Oh, Teddy. You've never been in my way. I'll be sad to see you go."

Laurie chuckled, a soft, sad sound that brought Jo down to her knees next to him.

"What is it?"

He turned to her, his tear-soaked face wrenching at her heart. "I've spent hours daydreaming about you sitting here, at this desk, writing your books, smiling when you noticed me sitting in the corner. Now my heart, that is already breaking with my grandfather's death, is breaking all over again with the pain of never knowing that memory."

"Teddy, you can't say such things," Jo cried and backed away from him. "I may not always get along with Amy, but she's my sister and I must speak up for her."

"What does Amy have to do with anything?"

"Aren't the two of you, well, something or other now?" Jo found the words hard to say and turned away from Laurie.

"Amy and I are nothing. Well, perhaps we are like brother and sister in some ways, but only on the best of days and certainly nothing more than that. Why are you saying this?"

"She told me she came to you and confessed her feelings to you. And all about how you asked her to go to Europe with you."

Laurie's eyes widened drastically. "Did she also tell you I told her there's only one woman in my heart and it isn't her? How I was going to Europe to get my mind off of you because I was so distraught from your last rejection that I needed to get away?"

Jo's heart raced, and she turned back around. "No." Her voice came out weak and she cleared her throat. "She failed to mention that part."

"Is that why you've been acting so strange?"

"Yes," Jo said slowly. "Why did you think?"

"I thought you were weirded out by your inheritance because you weren't sure how to kick me out of the house."

"Oh, heavens no, Teddy. I was quite relieved to know I'd have at least one person living here with me that I trust and love with my whole heart."

She reached out and grabbed Laurie's hand and he looked at her curiously.

"My fine fellow—I wish the situation around us wasn't so dismal and misunderstandings so abundant, but I have come to learn my heart more deeply—unfortunately due to fear—fear of losing you—that I must seize this opportunity before it doesn't come again, and my heart bursts or breaks entirely."

"Jo, what are you getting at?"

"My dearest Teddy." Jo looked into his eyes, wiping a stray tear from his cheek. "Life is much too short. I've learned that lesson so many times. Life is precious and I think the time is finally right."

Laurie looked up with a confused expression. "The time for what?"

"Let's get married."

"No, Jo. Don't." Laurie's face was contorted with pain and Jo felt the sting of tears at the corners of her own eyes.

"What? This is what you've always wanted." Jo ran her fingers through her hair and jumped to her feet. "What have I done wrong this time?"

"You've never done anything wrong, Jo. You've always been yourself. Perfectly yourself."

"Then why won't you let me do this?"

"Because you're either doing it out of fear or obligation. I haven't quite figured out which it is yet."

Jo dropped to the floor again and grabbed Laurie's hands. "No!" she cried. "The only obligation I feel towards you is one that is born of a deep, lasting friendship—one that I hope you feel for me, too. And as for fear. You know what fear has done? It has made me do foolish things like turn down your proposals." She squeezed his hands and bowed her head. "I don't deserve you, Teddy. You should've run the first time I said no to you. You should've run and never looked back. Now we're both sitting here, brokenhearted and in tears. We're a pathetic pair, but it isn't fear making me ask you to be my husband. It's—dare I say—*love*." The last word came out in a soft tone and astonished them both.

"Jo," Laurie breathed. "You mean *love* like the love I have always felt for you and not *love* like the way you've always felt for me?"

"My old fellow, I believe they're one and the same. It was that imprudent fear that made me believe otherwise. When I thought that Amy—" Jo closed her eyes against the pain. "When I thought I lost you forever, I recognized in that moment all the ways I had been wrong and all the ways I had been too stubborn."

"You would never lose me, not entirely anyway."

"Yes, but for the first time, I realized there is something quite different in having you all to myself." Jo scrunched her nose. "Maybe I'm selfish, but I can't share you with anyone else, Teddy. Not like that anyway."

Laurie threw his arms around Jo and buried his face in her neck. "Jo," he murmured. "Love is, in a way, selfish. Let us be selfish together and relish in this feeling before we tell the others tomorrow."

"So, is that a yes? Will you make me the happiest fellow to ever live and marry me?"

"A thousand times yes, Jo!" He smiled mischievously. "I should play coy and say no a few times but—" and here, Jo cut him off with a kiss more passionate than the world had ever known, filled with all the awkwardness one should expect from two lovers who have held back their love for so long—one willingly and one obligingly.

Jo smiled serenely and wondered why she had ever fought against this love. In that moment, she was certain she would never fight with her Teddy again. She was wrong, for their relationship was one born out of a mutual, otherworldly passion that sometimes warmed their hearts and sometimes burned their pride, but for that moment, all felt right and tranquil.

As they embraced and shared each other's joy and pain, a portrait of grandfather smiled down at the two of them. Jo couldn't believe she ever thought his eyes looked stern in it and it became her favorite painting of him they possessed.

17

S UMMER *1873*

"Three cheers for our favorite author!" Amy held up a glass and the family sitting around the table cheered heartily for Jo, who sat with a pleased smile on her face, though she tried to hide just how much the celebration meant to her.

"An instant classic, Little Women is certain to de-light readers of all ages for ages to come." Father held up the newspaper as he read a review that made Jo blush.

"Oh, now they don't know that." She ducked her head and tried to hide, but her fiancée hooked her chin with his thumb and tilted her head up.

"Believe in yourself, Jo!" Laurie cried and everyone cheered.

She smiled softly at him and resigned herself to bask in the glow from her family's praise. "This is the life I've always dreamed of and our wedding at the end of this week will be a triumphant conclusion to a long chapter filled with all sorts of adventures we never could have dreamed."

"Here's to new chapters with the best family I could have ever been sent to live next door to!" Laurie raised his cup with a rousing cheer and everyone joined in.

Jo looked around the table and her heart swelled with pride at each turn of her face. At one end sat father and Marmee, beaming with joy at their happiness and the happiness of their children, Meg and John wrapped up in little conversations with the twins who had stolen their hearts so completely, Amy who was currently caught up in a funny story with her fiancée, Fred Vaughn, and finally, Jo's eyes rested on her own fiancée and she was certain her heart would burst from the happiness she felt.

A few short days later, Marmee threw open the curtains in Jo's room to reveal perfect weather for the big day ahead. Jo awoke with a tender smile on her lips as she became conscious of the memory that she would marry her best friend in a matter of hours.

Her sisters came into the room and Jo was beyond grateful Marmee had asked them all to stay at Orchard House the night before the wedding. The entire evening had been spent sharing stories, laughter, and tears until it was time to retire to bed. It felt like one last hurrah before she started a new life, and Jo wouldn't have had it any other way.

They sat down on Jo's bed and began brushing her hair, singing the uplifting tunes they had spent their childhood warbling around the house.

The hours of preparation flew by faster than Jo would have liked and suddenly she found herself linking arms with her father, holding a bouquet of wildflowers in her hand, making her way down the aisle to Laurie.

She watched him as he turned and saw her. His face lit up brighter than the sun shining down on them, and her heart soared at the sight. He was like a breath of fresh air and made her feel so free and joyful. She could hardly imagine why she thought marrying him would be restrictive.

The past year of being engaged had been the best year of her life. Everything was coming together for her and she felt as if the world was hers to conquer. Having him by her side only amplified that feeling and made her burst with gratitude.

Laurie watched his bride walk down the aisle toward him, her eyes locked on his own, her hand gripping onto her father's arm and a shaky smile on her face.

She was content on a stage in costume and filled with lines from her imagination, but he could see her nerves were rattled being on such a prominent stage in such a vulnerable setting, with no character to hide behind. How he longed to comfort her and pull her up into his arms to take away those nerves and help her feel safe.

As soon as Jo was within steps of him, Laurie broke away from the altar and stepped forward to meet her. He took her shaky hand in his and felt it steady in his warm grasp.

The ceremony, all agreed, was the most beautiful they had ever seen. Eccentric, yet unassuming, like the bride and groom, the wedding left everyone with laughter and tears of joy streaking their faces as toasts to long life and happiness filled the air, along with toasts imagining what their dearly departed loved ones would say to know the two had finally found the love and happiness they deserved.

The happy couple made their rounds to each guest before getting lost in each other.

18

— • —

"**W**HAT A CONTENT LIFE this is." Jo shut the ocean air behind them as she closed the door to a summer cottage Marmee and Meg had arranged for their honeymoon. "I don't know that I could ever live inland again"

Laurie took her coat and hung it with his next to the door. "Me either. Concord is hardly that far inland, but these beaches of Plymouth seem like a different world entirely."

"Let's make sure we take more time to escape to places like this—just you and I."

"What a joy it would be to sit around the beach and do nothing. I could tinker on the piano while you write when it strikes you, but we wouldn't have to do anything we didn't want to."

"There's certainly no way we can sit around and do nothing for the rest of our days—I've learned my lessons there—but I do enjoy it when you fill the house with music and I must do something to make that your job."

"If I were to sell the businesses and make music for you the rest of my days, I should think I would be quite content to receive payment in the form of seeing you smile every morning when you awoke and every evening before your eyes closed."

Jo scrunched up her nose.

"Was that much too romantic for you?"

"Quite too much—" Jo hesitated and looked at Laurie sideways. "But, seeing as no one else is around, I will give you the indulgence of hearing me admit I liked it."

Laurie threw back his head and laughed heartily. He pulled Jo tight against him and pressed his lips to her forehead. "My sweet Jo. I knew there was a romantic old sap hiding somewhere in that heart of yours."

"Tell anyone and I'll make sure you're never able to speak again!" Her ferocious eyes made him laugh again, and she playfully shoved him back. "I'm serious! I have a reputation to uphold!"

Laurie kissed the top of her head and trailed his kisses down to her waiting mouth. "Jo," he said breathlessly, "let's live in this honeymoon state forever."

She laughed and fell back onto the couch, pulling Laurie down with her. "I have a wild idea. Why don't we purchase this cottage?"

"This one? Is it even for sale?"

"While you were napping yesterday, I took a short walk and ran into the owner. She's an older woman who manages a few houses and looked relieved at the prospect of selling one." She grabbed Laurie's shirt and smiled up at him. "It could be our wedding present to each other. I'd never once dreamed of being rich enough to own a summer home, but it's funny how right it feels."

"It does feel right. This cottage feels like a good place to call home when it's warm. Let's set up the arrangements before we leave here."

"It can be a summer home for the whole family. Can you imagine the twins running around? Meg would go mad keeping them back from the water, but John does a good job chasing them down."

"There's room enough that we could all come down at least once a year for a rousing family get together."

Jo interlaced her fingers with Laurie's and leaned her head against his chest. "That does sound delightful."

"Let's get some rest before we take a walk to enjoy tonight's sunset."

Laurie received no reply and looked down to see Jo sleeping soundly against him. He pressed his lips to her sun-kissed hair and closed his own eyes, drifting off into a peaceful dream filled with hopes and wishes for their future.

EPILOGUE

L AURIE KISSED THE TIPS of Jo's ink-stained fingers. "You have been up all night. Come to bed and solve the riddle of your story in the morning."

Jo looked from her paper to the man standing in front of her. His hair was disheveled and his eyes were heavy from waiting up for her. She set her pen down with a heavy sigh. "You should have gone to bed hours ago."

"I couldn't sleep knowing you were awake." His hand gently cradled the swell of her belly. "Can you believe she'll be here any day?"

"Here, help me up. *He* surely will be here any day." Jo reached out for Laurie's hands and hoisted herself up from her chair with the help of his steady grip.

"I can't help but wish to have a little girl with her mother's intense eyes, mischievous and playful nature, and spitfire spirit."

Jo turned to him, horrified. "No! I should hope *he* is a boy and not subject to all the restrictions and rules placed on girls!"

"My dear, sweet Jo! When will you see the good you do for this backwards, restrictive world of girls? If we are blessed with a little girl, you will be her first teacher that will show her the world is hers to conquer and I shall be her second. Together, we will show her that she can go out and make her own existence. What say you, my fellow?" His voice was soothing, and Jo leaned against him tenderly as he kissed the top of her head. "Shall we be a united front that knocks down the stone walls that threaten to destroy her?"

"Hmph," moaned Jo, unwilling to let on how much his speech touched her. "I still shall wish with all my heart that this babe is a boy."

Laurie noticed that, despite the scowl on her brow, Jo's eyes sparkled with hope as she cradled the swell of her belly and her voice had softened at the thought of her own sweet girl.

Jo leaned more heavily against her husband as they made their way to the bedroom. The walk down the hall wasn't a long one, and she was thankful to be next door to her mother so the two women could sensibly go about their lives instead of waiting around for something that seemed like it would never happen.

Her first step felt fine. The next hurt slightly, and the following was excruciating. She leaned against the wall and Laurie's eyes grew wide.

"Go get Marmee. Now!" Jo panted and pointed down the hall.

Sensibly, Laurie helped her take the next few aching steps and got her into their bedroom. As soon as she was safely on the bed, he sprinted over to the March house faster than he ever had any single day of his youth.

Laurie paced the halls and listened for signs of the door opening. When it finally unlatched, he rushed to meet Marmee. "How's Jo? Is the baby a boy or a girl?"

Marmee's eyes glistened with pride. "You'll have to see for yourself." She ushered him in the quiet room where Jo was laying against a fortress of pillows, holding a small bundle in her arms.

He rushed to her side and kissed her forehead with a depth of love that made Jo feel as if she melted into a puddle of happiness she never knew could exist.

"Teddy, meet our daughter, Elizabeth Margaret May Laurence!"

"Oh, Jo! You did a splendid job bringing our first sweet girl to us." He pressed his forehead to hers so they could look at their daughter from the same view. "I know you think you're not fit for this, but I strongly disagree!"

"For once, Teddy, I have no desire to argue with you! I am so wholly and completely in love with this girl and her father that I shall rise to the occasion and be my best possible self for the two of you!"

"You already are," Laurie said, softly, kissing Jo with a tenderness that brought Marmee to tears.

She softly backed out of the room and shut the door softly, not wanting to disturb such a precious moment for the newly formed family.

She leaned against the walls of the grand home, content that her most fiery daughter had found herself at last.

SWEPT AWAY AT SEASIDE POINT

Freshly free from an abusive marriage, Carla heads twelve hours from everything she's ever known to start over in a small coastal town called Seaside Point.

She answers an ad for a housekeeper and expects to find a woman waiting for her when she arrives. Instead, she's face-to-face with a grumpy, weathered fisherman named Kelly.

Determined to carve out a new future for herself, she does her best to make the situation work and befriends most of the town. She finds that Kelly isn't exactly who he first appeared to be and just when everything is coming together, her past shows up and threatens to destroy everything she has built.

Will Seaside Point be her safe refuge or will she need to keep running?

Read more: https://www.creekbound-books.com/taylor-claremont

**More Sweet, Happily-Ever-After
Books by Taylor Claremont**

*Love Found: Jo & Laurie – A Reimagined Little
Women Sequel*
Love in Lockwood
Plain Jane
Struck by Cupid
Entwined in Time Trilogy
The Necklace
Mackenzie Rising
Becoming Balfour
Christmas Stories
Christmas Trees & Cocoa
Merry Florida Christmas
Christmas by Design
A Christmas Story of Hope
Christmas Happily Ever After Collection
Seaside Point
Swept Away
Buried Storms
Something Blue
Find all of Taylor Claremont's titles at

www.TaylorClaremont.com

A Pacific Northwest native, Taylor Claremont travels the country at every opportunity she can with her loving husband and their two beautiful daughters.

When she's not playing board games or watching movies cuddled up with her family, her spare time is spent writing, reading, crocheting, and walking in nature.

She loves finding the extraordinary in the mundane and hopes to leave a glimmer of magic in everything she touches.

A lover of love stories and happy endings, Taylor Claremont writes stories that capture readers' hearts and etch a lasting hope into their souls.